Pizza for Sam

Written by **Mary Labatt**

Illustrated by **Marisol Sarrazin**

Kids Can Press

Text © 2003 Mary Labatt
Illustrations © 2003 Marisol Sarrazin

Kids Can Press acknowledges the financial support of the Ontario Arts Council, the Canada Council for the Arts and the Government of Canada, through the BPIDP, for our publishing activity.

Published in Canada by
Kids Can Press Ltd.
29 Birch Avenue
Toronto, ON M4V 1E2

Published in the U.S. by
Kids Can Press Ltd.
2250 Military Road
Tonawanda, NY 14150

www.kidscanpress.com

Edited by David MacDonald
Designed by Stacie Bowes and Marie Bartholomew
Printed in Hong Kong, China.

The hardcover edition of this book is smyth sewn casebound.
The paperback edition of this book is limp sewn with a drawn-on cover.

CM 03 0 9 8 7 6 5 4 3 2 1
CM PA 03 0 9 8 7 6 5 4 3 2 1

National Library of Canada Cataloguing in Publication Data

Labatt, Mary, 1944–
    Pizza for Sam / written by Mary Labatt ; illustrated by Marisol Sarrazin.

(Kids can read)
ISBN 1-55337-329-4 (bound).   ISBN 1-55337-331-6 (pbk.)

I. Sarrazin, Marisol, 1965– II. Title. III. Series: Kids Can read (Toronto, Ont.)

PS8573.A135P59 2003   jC813'.54
C2002-901431-X PZ7

Kids Can Press is a *CORUS*™ Entertainment company

Joan and Bob were having a party.

They made food.

No one made food for Sam.

The doorbell rang.

Joan and Bob ran to the door.

Sam ran, too.

Sam saw cake and cookies

and pie and chips.

"This is good," thought Sam.

"I need food."

Joan and Bob put the food

on the table.

Sam sniffed.

"YUM!" thought Sam.

"This is good food."

Sam jumped on a chair.

She sniffed the cake.

"I like cake," thought Sam.

"Cake is good for puppies."

But Bob saw her.

"NO, Sam!" he cried.

"Cake is not for puppies!"

"Woof!" said Sam.

She flopped on the floor.

"I need food.

I need food for puppies."

Sam jumped back

on the chair.

She sniffed the cookies.

"I like cookies," thought Sam.

"Cookies are good for puppies."

But Joan saw her.

"NO, Sam!" she cried.

"Cookies are not for puppies."

"Woof!" said Sam.

She flopped on the floor.

"I need food.

I need food for puppies."

Sam jumped back

on the chair.

She sniffed the pie.

"I like pie," thought Sam.

"Pie is good for puppies."

But Joan and Bob saw her.

"NO, Sam!" they cried.

"Pie is not for puppies!"

"Woof!" said Sam.

She flopped on the floor.

"I need food.

I need food for puppies!"

Sam went to her bowl.

She put her chin on her paws.

She closed her eyes

and started to dream.

Sam dreamed of cake

and cookies

and pie and chips.

Lots of chips!

Bob came back.

Sam opened her eyes.

"Are you hungry, Sam?" he asked.

Sam jumped up.

"You bet!" she thought.

"Bring on the food."

Bob went to the kitchen.

He came back

with Sam's bowl.

Sam sniffed.

"YUCK!" thought Sam.

"This is dog food!"

"Dog food stinks!

I hate dog food!"

Sam was sad.

"Dog food is NOT for puppies!"

The doorbell rang.

Joan and Bob ran to the door.

Sam ran, too.

A man had a big box.

"Pizza!" said the man.

Sam sniffed and sniffed.

"What is pizza?" thought Sam.

"It does not smell

like cake or cookies.

It does not smell

like pie or chips.

Best of all,

it does NOT smell like dog food!"

Joan put the box on the table.

The doorbell rang.

The telephone rang, too.

Joan went one way.

Bob went the other way.

Sam looked at the box.

She looked around.

Everyone was busy.

Sam dragged the box

behind the sofa.

She scratched the box

and chewed the box.

"Gr-r-r-r."

At last, the box was open!

Sam took a big bite.

"YUM!" she thought.

"This is good food!"

"Cake is not for puppies.

Cookies are not for puppies.

Pie is not for puppies.

Dog food is not for puppies.

I know what is for puppies ..."

"Pizza is for puppies!"